# NABBED IN NEW MEXICO

RAMBLING RV COZY MYSTERIES, BOOK 6

## PATTI BENNING

D1523209

SUMMER PRESCOTT BOOKS PUBLISHING

# CHAPTER ONE

"I'll be back before you know it."

Planting a last kiss on his shiny black beak, Tulia Blake pulled back and watched as the vet tech shut the cage door. Cicero, her African grey parrot, let out a sharp whistle, puffing out his feathers as a warning to the stranger getting close to him. The cage latched with a click, and the vet tech turned to her, a smile on her face.

"He'll be just fine. We board parrots all the time. He might be a little nervous at first, but soon he'll be chatting away with the other birds. We've even got another African grey in—I'm sure he'll love whistling back and forth to her."

Tulia looked where the other woman gestured.

Sure enough, a few feet away, a parrot was hanging on the bars of its cage, already observing Cicero with interest. The bird was slightly smaller than him, and darker, with dark grey feathers and a maroon tail to his dark red one. She recognized it as the rarer subspecies, the Timneh African grey.

The sound of claws on metal made her look back around to Cicero, who was climbing on the bars of his own cage, his pale eyes pinning as he looked at the other bird. When he whistled, the other bird responded, mirroring the noise, and Tulia smiled. She felt guilty about leaving him here while she went on a two-day hike, but it seemed like he would be just fine.

"I'm glad he'll have company," she said, waving goodbye to him one last time—not that he was paying attention to her anymore—and following the tech back to the clinic's reception area. "Call me if anything happens, all right? Even if he just seems upset—I'll just be a phone call away."

The vet tech assured her once again that everything would be fine. Feeling like a nervous parent leaving her child at school for the first time, Tulia shot one last look back over her shoulder at the parrot boarding room before she left the exotic animal clinic. The bright New Mexico sun greeted her, and she squinted against the glare as she made her way toward her RV.

She had parked the vehicle awkwardly along the back of the parking lot. It was really too big for the space, especially with her sedan hooked to the back of it, but the stop had only taken her a few minutes. Tamping down the concern for Cicero—she had done her research, and this was one of the best exotic animal clinics in the area with plenty of good reviews from their boarding clients—she let herself into the RV and hit the button to start it up. The diesel engine rumbled to life, and after some careful maneuvering, she pulled out onto the road.

As she left the vet clinic behind, the worry and guilt she felt for leaving her bird behind changed into a tingle of excitement. She'd scheduled an overnight hike into the New Mexico wilds with a tour company. They weren't far from the infamous Roswell, and while the chance to spot a UFO was one of the company's advertising points, she didn't really expect to see any aliens. No, what she was excited about was the trip itself.

Born and raised in green, humid Michigan, New Mexico's arid climate was new to her. She'd spent the last couple of days driving through similar surroundings, but she hadn't wanted to risk going hiking on her own. The environment was so different than what she was used to, she hadn't wanted to take the risk of getting injured and lost, or stumbling across the wrong sort of venomous creature with the nearest help miles away. The tour company should be safe, though. They were relatively new, according to their website, but all their reviews over the year they had been open had been good.

This would be something new for her to do, and it felt good to be branching out. Plus, there was the added benefit of the hike taking place in the absolute middle of nowhere. Luis, her ex-boyfriend turned stalker, wouldn't have a chance of finding her, if he was even in the state. Samuel, a friend she had made during her road trip who was a private investigator, was trying to track Luis down, but hadn't had any luck so far.

She pushed the thoughts of her ex away and focused on following the feminine voice of her phone's GPS as it directed her to the tour company's headquarters. She'd called ahead and had been assured that there was space for her to park her RV overnight—in fact, the overnight parking was included in the fee she had paid to reserve the tour—

but she was still a little worried about it until she came to the final turnoff.

They had plenty of space for parking, that much was evident, but the sight of the tiny, beat-up metal building standing in the middle of a wide-open expanse of hard red earth and spiky plants gave her a new sort of worry. It didn't exactly look like the most official base of operations for what was supposed to be a reputable tour company.

Biting her lower lip, she pulled in and parked on a hard-packed expanse of earth near a few other vehicles. She saw a woman getting out of a hybrid electric vehicle with a large pink backpack, and a man was leaning against a truck with a more functional looking hiking pack resting at his feet. There were some other people gathered closer to the building, which made her feel better; if she had been the only one there, she probably would have driven right past the place.

Still, she hesitated, letting the engine idle as she tried to reassure herself that the tour would be safe. There would be other people in the group—she had specifically wanted to go in a group, instead of opting for an individual tour—and the tour company *had* received good reviews. The sight of a man approaching her driver's side door made up her mind for her, and she shut the engine off and got out of the RV.

"Hello, my name is Ricardo Sia," he said, shaking her hand. His accent had a slight Hispanic tinge to it. "I talked to you on the phone when you called about the RV."

"I remember," she said, smiling. "Is this an okay place to park it?"

"It's fine," he assured her. "We are the only tour group leaving until the end of the week. Pack your things up, lock your vehicle, and come on over to the base to get checked in. I need to make sure you've packed everything on the list we emailed you when you paid. Even in a tour group, it's dangerous to go into the desert without the proper supplies."

"Right. I made sure I bought everything, but I'll double-check that I have it all packed into my bag."

When he walked away to go talk with the woman who was struggling with her pink backpack, Tulia climbed back into the RV and took the hiking back-pack she had bought a few days ago out from under her bed. It was a professional-looking piece of equip-ment, with a metal frame and a bunch of straps that were supposed to help distribute the weight across her body to make carrying it easier. And it certainly weighed quite a bit. The list she had received included a lot of water, more than she could possibly need for a two-day hike. She also had extra food, fire-starting supplies, a one-person tent, a mirror and a brightly colored strip of cloth for signaling emergency rescue services, and among other things, a warm jacket. It could get cold at night, apparently. With the sun beating down like it was, it was hard to imagine needing it, but she'd packed it anyway.

She double-checked that she had everything on the list, then carefully packed her keys and her wallet into a zipped pocket inside the backpack. Her phone went into her pocket along with her pepper spray, and she hid her purse under her bed. She only wanted to worry about carrying one bag.

Then, she hefted the pack, staggering slightly under its weight. She felt a moment of trepidation. Could she do this? Had she overestimated her level of fitness? She shifted around, tightening some straps and hitching the bag up higher on her back. The weight settled a bit, and she knew it would be better once she clipped the waist band over her hips. And as she used her water, the bag would begin to get lighter.

She could do this. She knew she could. She might be sore and sweaty, and her back might complain for a few days afterward, but she wasn't going to back out just because it would be hard.

After one last look around the RV to make sure she wasn't forgetting anything, she climbed down. She had to pause to unzip the backpack for her keys because she had zipped them up too soon, but then the RV was locked. She settled the bag back over her shoulders and strode off to find Ricardo and prove she was ready for the hike.

# CHAPTER TWO

Ricardo and the others were by the small metal building. He was just finishing up going through the other woman's list, and she had begun packing her items away. It looked like they had six people total, including Ricardo, their guide. There was only one other woman besides Tulia, and she had a pinched expression on her face as she put her things back in her bag that made Tulia feel as if she should wait to introduce herself. Instead, she turned to the man beside her. He had his bag strapped to his back and looked ready to go; Ricardo must have already cleared him.

"Hi, I'm Tulia," she said. "Is this your first tour like this?"

"Alan," he said, shaking her hand. "I'm from

Vermont, and I hike a lot there. I'm here for a work convention, but it doesn't start until Wednesday. Thought I'd get some of the tourist stuff out of the way first thing. You?"

"I'm from Michigan," she told him. "I've never done anything like this before. The most I've hiked is a few miles. But I think I'm ready."

"It might be tough in parts, but that's part of what makes it worth it."

She nodded her agreement then stepped forward when Ricardo called her name. They went through each and every item on the checklist. He was thorough, making sure she had enough of everything and hadn't cut corners. His seriousness was starting to make her worry again; was this hike more dangerous than she expected, or was Ricardo just being cautious? He *was* responsible for all five of them. She supposed she couldn't blame him for wanting to make sure nothing went wrong.

Once he was through the checklist, he nodded at her and then said, "That's all of us. You've all signed your release forms already. The plan is to hike six miles out to Rattler Plateau, camp out, swing around to the Green Man Oasis, and make our way back at a more relaxed pace the next day. We'll be back here by the evening after tomorrow, unless something delays us."

"What sort of delays are you expecting?" the other woman asked.

"I'm not expecting any delays. The weather is supposed to be clear the next few days, but that doesn't mean it's impossible we'll get an unexpected storm. If someone gets injured, it will also delay us. We move at the pace of our slowest walker. Remember that—we don't leave anyone behind. Stick to the group. Don't go touching snakes or scorpions, don't fool around on rock formations. Remember that a lot of the flora and fauna you'll see is protected; be respectful, keep your distance, and don't leave a mark on the environment besides your footprints. Use common sense. I've done this hike nearly twenty times, and it's a pretty safe one, but that doesn't mean it's impossible that something unexpected will happen. The desert does kill people every year. Don't be afraid, but keep it in mind."

There was some subdued murmuring in the group, and Tulia shifted on her feet. She felt a little nervous, but also excited, and it seemed like everyone else felt the same way too. Beside her, Alan bounced on his toes.

"All right, I'm going to contact my boss and let

her know we're heading out and when we plan to be back. We've got cell service right here, but won't when we get out there, so if there's any calls anyone has to make, do it now. This is also your last chance to use the facilities—once we leave, you'll be stuck using a hole in the dirt until we get back. Otherwise, chat amongst yourselves, get to know each other. We'll head out as soon as I'm off the phone."

He nodded to them, then entered the building, already pulling his cell phone out of his pocket. Tulia wasn't sure what to do—she didn't have to use the bathroom, and didn't have anyone to call. She'd already told her parents about her trip and had mentioned it to Samuel as well, so he wouldn't worry if he tried to call her but couldn't reach her. No one else rushed to make any last calls either, and Alan turned to one of the other men nearby to introduce himself. That seemed to break the ice, because soon they were doing introductions all around.

Tulia hadn't realized it before, but as she talked to the others, she realized there were no couples or friends. No one here knew each other. It struck her as odd, but it did mean people were more interested in going out of their way to be friendly than they might have been if they were with friends or family.

She'd already met Alan, with his slightly stringy

dark brown hair and habit of bouncing on his toes when he was eager, but now she learned that the man she first saw, who had been leaning against his truck when she pulled in, was named Noah. He seemed quiet, not giving much more than his name and the fact that he was a local. His brown hair was graying, and his shirt had a hole in the back of one shoulder. She didn't point it out to him.

The third man was named Cristan Segura and seemed short and to the point. He looked into the building after Ricardo with narrowed eyes, running a hand through his short black hair in an action that seemed to be an involuntary tic.

The woman introduced herself as Rosemary, and whatever had her in a bad mood earlier seemed to have passed, because she smiled brightly and seemed eager to chat Tulia's ear off as they waited.

"My sister is a nature photographer," Rosemary said. "She's always taking all sorts of gorgeous pictures. I'm stuck in an office all day, or I used to be, so now that I have the opportunity, I wanted to take the chance to get out and enjoy the scenery myself. I already feel better than I have in months. Who knew getting out of that cubicle would be a cure-all?"

"Did you get a different job?" Tulia asked, curious.

"Not exactly." Rosemary looked around, but no one else was paying attention to them. She brushed a section of her hair behind her ears; it was blonde and neatly trimmed, with darker roots. Lowering her voice, she leaned in closer to Tulia. "I won a lawsuit against my old employer. It's not enough money to retire on, but it's enough for me to take a break, regroup, and figure out what I want to do from here on out."

Tulia raised an eyebrow, even more curious now, but she knew it would be far from appropriate to ask what the lawsuit had been about. Ricardo came out of the building at that moment, his own backpack strapped to his back, saving her from having to think of a response.

"Everyone ready? Let's get going. Don't be shy to speak up if you need me to slow down. We've got plenty of time to reach our destination before nightfall."

They started walking away from the road and the building. Tulia shot one last glance back at her RV, then turned her attention forward. Whatever path Ricardo was following wasn't evident to her eyes, but he seemed confident that he knew where he was going, which gave her confidence. She fell into step just behind Rosemary and tried to focus on the scenery, not the weight of the bag on her back or the sun beating down on her head. It really was beautiful out here, in a harsh and lonely sort of way.

In her pocket, her phone buzzed. Frowning, she pulled it out, a surge of worry going through her at the thought that it might be the vet's office, calling about Cicero. But the area code was from California. Samuel? Last she heard, he was still in San Francisco, but she couldn't think of why he would be calling from an unknown number. Dropping back even farther so she had some semblance of privacy, she pressed the phone to her ear.

"Hello?"

"Hello, am I speaking with Tulia Blake?" The man's voice was crisp and professional, and did nothing to ease the knot of worry in her stomach.

"This is she."

"This is Burt Damon." He named the hotel she had stayed at in San Francisco the week before, and she recognized his name. He was the hotel's manager. "I'm giving you a courtesy call to let you know your fiancé recently came in, looking for you. It's our policy not to give out private information about our guests, but I did agree to pass a call on to the number we last had on file. It seemed urgent."

"My fiancé?" she asked, her voice catching. "Did he give his name?"

"He didn't, ma'am. I apologize. He left when I pressed him for more information. I thought you ought to know."

"Thank you," she said, her voice tight. "I don't have a fiancé. I think I know who he is, though. Please don't tell him anything about me. Tell your employees too, if you can."

"I will." He sounded concerned now. "Should I contact the police? I admit, the interaction seemed strange to me."

"No," she said after a moment's hesitation. "I've got someone working on it already. I'm glad you called me."

She ended the call a moment later, adrenaline making her fingers shake as she typed out a text message to Samuel. *Luis was at the hotel. He was looking for me, the manager let me know. Hope you're still in the area. Let me know if you find him. Heading out on my hike, don't worry if you can't contact me until tomorrow.*

She considered adding some Xs or Os, but their relationship wasn't quite there yet. She left the message at that and hit send, watching to make sure it went through before she put her phone in her pocket and hurried to catch up with the others. Rosemary shot her a questioning glance, but Tulia shook her head. She didn't want to explain the whole convoluted mess, especially not when it meant revealing her biggest secret.

The fewer people who knew she was a lottery winner, the better.

# CHAPTER THREE

She tried to put Luis out of her mind as she followed Ricardo and the rest of the group into the New Mexico desert. She tried to tell herself that it was a good thing, knowing for a fact that Luis was still in another state. It would take him more than a couple hours to make it from San Francisco to the Roswell area, and that was if he even knew where she was—which it didn't seem as if he did. She was updating her blog on a delay now, and wouldn't post about this hike until she had already reached her next destination. With any luck, it would take him a long time to figure out what she was doing, and she could keep him one step behind her that way.

A few people chatted as they walked, and it became evident Cristan knew Ricardo. They laughed and joked like old friends, occasionally talking together in low voices at the front of the group, too quiet for the others to hear. Once, Cristan looked back and gave the group an almost smug smile. Ricardo elbowed him, and he fell back with the rest of them.

When they stopped half an hour later to drink water and take pictures of a lizard Alan had spotted on a rock, Tulia checked her phone. Her single bar of service had vanished, leaving her without a way to contact the outside world. At least the message to Samuel had gone through, but he would have no way to get back to her until she returned. He was capable, though, and she knew he would figure something out if he did manage to track down Luis. Unlike her ex, she had every faith in him.

They arrived at their first campsite when the sun was just beginning to dip toward the horizon, the angle of the light through the atmosphere making it look bigger and redder than she was used to. They had been hiking toward a rock formation for the past couple hours, and now they were at the base of it. It was a small, rocky plateau with a couple of scraggly trees clinging to the side. Ricardo let them stop for another short break at the base of it, then they began to climb. She could see the path worn through the dirt here, and tried to step where the others stepped, not wanting to twist an ankle and be the reason everyone got home late.

When she got to the top, she paused to stare. The plateau wasn't very tall, more a flat hill than anything, but the view of the flat landscape all around them was impressive. She couldn't see the road—any road— from here, and couldn't see any buildings either. It was all just nature. Sand, dirt, rocks, and plants, with the desert's animal denizens hidden away in their natural habitat.

It was getting windy, either due to the rise in elevation, small though it was, or due to the evening's changing temperature. Ricardo showed them a clear patch of ground that had obviously been used for camping before, with a fire pit already dug out and space cleared of rocks and sticks, and all of them set down their packs with a relieved group sigh. Tulia stretched. Her muscles felt like jelly. She just knew that loose, wobbly feeling was going to turn into soreness the next day.

"It's time to start setting up the tents," Ricardo said. "We'll eat after. No fire, remember. There's a burn ban in the area. Trust me when I tell you, you want to have your tents set up *before* you sit down to eat. Your muscles will stiffen when you stop moving, and the last thing you'll want to do with stiff muscles, sore feet, and a full stomach will be to wrestle with a tent in the dark."

They all took his advice to heart, splitting up to claim their own small patches of ground. Rosemary took a spot next to Tulia. As the only two women in the group, Tulia felt a sense of solidarity with her, and the other woman seemed to return it, even though they didn't seem to have much in common.

Tulia got her tent set up without much issue, and inside, she laid out the thin sleeping bag that claimed to be extra lightweight and designed especially for backpacking. She hadn't brought a pad or any thick blankets to lay on, not wanting to weigh herself down. That had probably been the right decision, but it was still a trade-off between having a sore back from carrying too much and having a sore back from sleeping on the hard ground. She'd live, though; she was only sleeping rough for two nights.

She propped her backpack up on the ground outside her tent and took out some water and her meal for tonight. She'd snacked on a granola bar earlier, but the thought of actually having warm food made her stomach growl. The others must have been just as hungry, because everyone migrated to the center of camp as soon as their tents were assembled. Before long, they were gathered on large rocks and branches they could use as makeshift seats, and the sky was turning a beautiful orange pink as the sun sank down past the horizon.

They ate, then sat and talked, the pale light of the battery-powered lanterns casting strange shadows on their faces. It made the night feel strange, almost dreamlike. Finally, when the sun had gone completely down, without even a hint of its light on the horizon, Ricardo turned off all of the lanterns and bade them to look up.

Tulia did so, and couldn't tear her eyes away. She had been camping in some pretty remote places over these past few months, but there had always been trees, or the glow of a city off in the distance. Here, nothing interrupted her view of the stars. There was just the dark expanse of the desert and then the endless sprawl of lights in the sky.

"I think I saw a UFO!" Rosemary's exclamation brought Tulia back down to earth, and she looked at the other woman, who was pointing off into the distance. "Look, there it is again."

Everyone's heads turned, and after a few seconds, Tulia saw a faint light speed through the sky, burning bright only to vanish a moment later.

Ricardo chuckled, not unkindly, but as if he was used to this happening. "Those are shooting stars.

Make a wish. In fact, make a lot of them. You'll see quite a few of them out here."

Even though she knew it was silly and superstitious, Tulia waited until she saw another light dash across the sky, then thought, *I wish Luis would stop trying to find me.* Then, feeling guilty about not wishing for something more selfless, she found another one and wished good health and happiness for her family and friends.

They stargazed for a while, with a handful more false UFO sightings, one of which turned out to be an airplane. It was fun. Tulia didn't think anyone was taking it too seriously, but there, under the stars, in the middle of the desert, there was the slightest sense that something *might* happen. As far as Tulia was concerned, it was a great evening. Still, she was tired, and her muscles were stiff and sore from the day of hard exercise, so when Noah, who was the only one who hadn't made any alien jokes, got up and went to his tent, she made her excuses as well and got up.

After dragging her backpack inside the tent, she zipped it up and then sat on top of her sleeping bag. It was dark, but she didn't want to distract from the stargazing for everyone else, so she didn't turn on the small lantern she had brought. Instead, she used the light from her phone's screen to locate her pajamas.

Changing inside the tent was awkward, but she managed it. Once she was done, she climbed into the sleeping bag and stared up at the faint light coming in through the tent from the stars. She could hear the quiet murmur of conversation from the others, but couldn't make out any words. Somewhere to her right someone—Noah—started snoring. She closed her eyes, sleep coming to her easier than she thought it would.

When she woke up, it was still dark. She went from sleep to awareness in a second, and just lay there, her heart pounding in her chest. Had she had a nightmare? She couldn't remember having one, but *something* had woken her.

She reached for her phone and tapped the screen to wake it up so she could see the time, but the screen remained dark, and she remembered she had turned it off to conserve the battery. It didn't seem worth the effort to turn it on, since it didn't really matter what the time was. The sun wasn't up, which meant she should go back to sleep. That was really all she had to know.

She turned over, closing her eyes, but she still felt wide awake. Something rustled outside of her tent, and someone mumbled something in their sleep. She felt hyperaware of every sound, and nearly stopped breathing when she heard a man's voice say something in a low mutter. She chided herself; she was surrounded by people who had been perfectly friendly. She shouldn't be so jumpy.

When the man spoke again, she frowned. She couldn't make out what he was saying. He sounded too far away, which didn't make sense unless someone had decided to wander around in the dark. Something about the cadence of the man's voice sounded like he was having a conversation with someone, but she only heard one person talking. There wasn't any phone service out here—she had checked during dinner—so what was going on?

She sat up, tempted to unzip her tent and peek out just to assuage her curiosity, but before she could move, she heard a loud shout and the sound of rocks tumbling down a slope. Something crashed through the dry, scraggly brush. A moment later, she heard a woman's scream.

# CHAPTER FOUR

Tulia scrambled out of her tent, kicking her sleeping bag off and leaving the tent door open as she hurried toward the sound of the scream. She could see a person's dark silhouette at the edge of the plateau. Behind her, someone turned on a lantern, and in the light it cast, she saw Rosemary staring down over the edge of the plateau, her hair wild and her lips pulled back in a grimace.

"What happened?" Tulia asked, wishing she had thought to grab her own lantern. Whoever had thought to turn theirs on was hurrying toward them, but the movement made the shadows dance and leap.

"Someone fell," Rosemary said. She extended a shaking finger. "Down there."

Tulia looked over the edge of the plateau. It

wasn't quite sheer here, but it was close, and the side of the hill was covered in loose stones and rocks. There was a dead tree clinging to the side of the plateau partway down. She could just see its darker shape against the lighter rocks. What she didn't see was a person.

"What's going on?"

She turned to see Alan holding a lantern. Back at the campsite, she heard the sound of a tent unzipping and more voices.

"Someone fell," Rosemary said again. "Shine the light over."

Alan held the lantern out over the edge, and the three of them looked down. The lantern's light faded quickly, but it was enough to see a crumpled form at the bottom of the hill.

"Oh my goodness," Rosemary said, turning away. "I can't look. Is he all right?"

"Hey!" Alan called down. "Are you okay?"

There was no answer. Tulia turned at the sound of footsteps behind them, and saw Noah and Cristan approaching. Noah rubbed his red-rimmed eyes and blinked sleepily. Cristan looked annoyed.

"What's all this commotion?" Cristan asked.

"Someone fell down the hill," Rosemary said again.

"It has to have been Ricardo," Tulia added, looking around at everyone a second time, though she already knew his was the only face missing. "He's not responding when we call down to him."

The latecomers pushed forward, looking down with their lanterns and calling out much like Alan had done but without any better results. Tulia felt a cold ball of fear slowly growing in her stomach.

"We have to get down to him," Cristan said at last. "Does anyone have a strong blanket? We might need to use it to carry him. Is his backpack still up here? I think he has a first aid kit in it."

Alan volunteered his blanket, and Cristan found the first aid kit. Tulia took the chance to get her lantern from her tent and zip up the tent door, then their group began the careful treck down from the top of the small plateau. It wasn't very far, but the narrow path they had traversed during the day was a lot more treacherous at night. Twice, Tulia stumbled on a loose rock, and once she had to reach out to steady Rosemary when she tripped.

Once they reached the bottom of the plateau, they had to treck halfway around the base to find the place where Ricardo had fallen. This was hard going in a different way, since they were going off the path. Spiky plants tore at Tulia's pajama bottoms, and she was terrified that at any moment a snake was going to strike at her leg.

Finally, she saw Ricardo's still form at the bottom of the plateau. Cristan, who had taken the lead during all of this, probably since he had known Ricardo prior to the hike, hurried forward. He set his lantern down next to his friend and carefully reached for him.

Tulia reached them and held her lantern up, wanting to give him as much light as possible. It didn't look good, and she felt her heart sinking further as Cristan readjusted his fingers on the pulse point on Ricardo's neck. He gave up after a few seconds and reached for the man's wrist. After a long moment, he shook his head, looking up at the small group gathered around him.

"I can't find a pulse. I think he's dead."

Tulia stared at Ricardo, willing him to breathe. He would have tumbled down the hill, not fallen straight down since it wasn't sheer. Surely, that was something someone could survive? But he had a bloody gash on his head, and his legs were bent under him at uncomfortable angles. He wasn't moving. Alan tried to find a pulse too, and gave up quicker than Cristan did. He stood up, brushing the hand that had touched Ricardo's body off on his pants.

"What do we do?" he asked.

"We've got to carry him back up the plateau," Cristan said.

"That's a bad idea," Noah said, chiming in instead of simply watching grimly as he had been up until then. "We all almost slipped at least once coming down. It's going to be even more dangerous carrying a body up. It's dark, the path up to the top of the plateau is narrow, and we don't even have a proper stretcher."

"We can't just leave him here," Rosemary said. She was standing a distance back, staring at the body in horror. "What if something eats him?"

"We can cover him with my blanket," Alan suggested. "In the morning, maybe we can carry him out."

"All the way back to where our cars are? That's miles," Noah said.

"We can take turns," Alan argued.

"It's a bad idea. How are you even expecting to make it back without him?" Noah asked. "He was our guide. I think we should just stay put. We're expected back the day after tomorrow, and when we don't show up, someone will come looking for us."

"You want us to just wait here?" Rosemary asked. "What if we run out of water? And what are we going to do with ... with him?" She pointed at Ricardo, though she still seemed barely able to look at him. "We're supposed to sleep up there while he's lying down here, covered by nothing but a blanket?"

"Enough," Cristan snapped. "All of you, just be quiet. We don't have to decide anything tonight. In the morning, we can see if we can follow our tracks back out. Maybe just one person can go to get help and the others can wait here. Either way, I don't think it's a good idea to try to move Ricardo. The authorities are going to want to investigate and make sure no foul play was involved. If we move him, it could look like we're hiding something, like maybe his fall wasn't an accident."

"Are we sure it was?" Tulia asked, joining the argument she had to this point kept out of. "I heard a man's voice before he fell. It sounded like he was talking to someone. I don't think he was alone up there."

No one responded right away. Tulia saw Alan shoot a distrustful glance at Noah, and Cristan was frowning at her and Rosemary.

"One of you found him, didn't you?" he asked. "How did you know someone had fallen?"

"I heard him shout," Tulia said. "Something woke me up, and I was lying in my tent in the dark. That was when I heard the voice, and a moment later, a man's shout. That must have been when he went over the edge. A few moments later, I heard Rosemary scream."

Rosemary had been nodding along. "I heard him shout too. I went over to see—"

"You were out of your tent?" Cristan asked, suspicion lacing his voice.

"I had to use the restroom. Er, use a bush, in this case."

"I see," he said. "You heard him shout, but you didn't see him fall, then you went to look over the edge." She nodded. His lips pressed together. "Then, why did you scream?"

Rosemary blinked, taking half a step back from him. "What do you mean, why did I scream? I realized what must have happened, and I panicked."

It was Tulia's turn to frown. "When I asked you what had happened, you said 'Someone fell,' not 'I think someone fell.' You sounded pretty certain."

"What are you trying to say?" Rosemary asked, looking between her and Cristan. "Are you accusing me of pushing him?"

"I'm just not sure your story lines up," Cristan said. Tulia thought he was going to pursue it, but he shook his head sharply. "Enough. We'll figure it out later. Someone help me with the blanket. We don't want to move him too much, but I want to at least cover him. Whatever happened or didn't happen— we'll figure it out tomorrow. I don't think anyone is thinking clearly right now." He hesitated, then added. "I want to let it be known that I do have a gun, for self-protection. If someone did kill Ricardo, you'd better think twice about trying the same with anyone else."

# CHAPTER FIVE

Tulia didn't want to help Cristan tuck the blanket around Ricardo's body, but she knew no one else did either, so when no one stepped up to offer their aid in the first few moments, she volunteered.

It felt wrong to tuck the blanket around the man's head and shoulders. It felt even worse to help Cristan carry a few heavy rocks to pin the blanket down so the wind wouldn't tug it away. Finally, they finished, and Tulia wiped her dusty hands off on her pajama pants. She tried not to resent the others when she turned around to see that they had been watching, but hadn't once piped up to offer help themselves.

As much as she hated it, she knew she had more experience around dead bodies than most. She couldn't blame them for not wanting to get close. If this helped them sleep at night without nightmares, she wouldn't complain about her and Cristan doing all the work.

They made their way back up to the campsite and stood in silence for a moment until Alan said, "We might as well try to sleep. We'll figure everything out in the morning."

Their group broke apart with only a few mutters of 'goodnight.' Tulia zipped herself up in her tent, sipped some water, then lay down on her sleeping bag, her head pillowed against her backpack. She felt stunned. Numb. She was half tempted to go back outside and find a shooting star so she could wish this was all a dream. Instead, she closed her eyes, wondering if she would ever manage to get back to sleep.

She didn't know when she drifted off, but when she woke up, the pale light of dawn illuminated her tent. She stretched, reached for her phone out of reflex, remembered that it was off, then remembered everything else that had happened during the night.

Her stomach clenched. She got dressed quickly, grabbed some water and her toothbrush, and left the tent to find a private area to take care of her morning needs. A spiky bush provided the cover she needed. After she brushed her teeth and splashed some water on her face, she felt a little better, and returned to her tent to grab some food. Despite everything that had happened, she was still hungry; her body was probably still compensating for all of the exercise the day before.

When she exited her tent with a caffeine pill, a bottle of water, a granola bar, and some jerky, she saw Rosemary sitting on one of the big rocks, brushing out her hair slowly as she stared off into the desert. Alan was up, looking the opposite direction—the direction they had come. She didn't see the other two men, and tried to be quiet in case they were still sleeping.

She sat on a flat rock, downed her caffeine pill—a substitute for her regular hot cup of coffee, and began eating a strip of the peppered jerky she had brought. Alan glanced over his shoulder at the sound of her granola wrapper crinkling and came to join her when he spotted her. He sat near her, idly picking up a stone and fiddling with it. He glanced toward Rosemary, who was ignoring both of them.

"We should get going soon."

She looked up at him, surprised. "You still want to try to walk back without Ricardo? Aren't we supposed to stay where we are if we get lost?"

"Well, we aren't lost, are we? We know where we

are, and we know what direction we came from. I bet we'll be able to pick up on whatever path Ricardo was following."

"Bad idea," Cristan said from behind Tulia. She started; she hadn't heard him come up. He must have been down the path that led from the plateau to the ground, because she hadn't seen him when she looked around earlier. "There isn't just one path from the parking lot to here. There's hundreds."

"What do you mean?" Tulia asked.

"Game trails," he said. "People hiking, running. People drive four-wheelers out here and leave tracks behind. We might start out on the right path, but a mile in, we could end up following a trail to a coyote pack's favorite watering hole."

"Couldn't we just follow our footprints?" Alan asked. "It's not like coyotes wear hiking boots."

"What footprints?" Cristan raised an eyebrow. "Didn't you hear the wind last night? You really think you'll be able to find a single track down below? Don't bother looking; I already checked. Our prints are gone."

"Well, I don't want to just wait here for a rescue," Alan said. "We still know which direction we came from. As long as we head roughly the right way, we'll hit the road at some point. I know Ricardo's got to have a compass."

"Right, well, say you go through his stuff and find his compass. Which direction are you going to go?"

"That way," Alan said confidently, pointing. "I remember the angle we came at the plateau from."

"Right, but what direction is that?" Cristan asked. "North? East?" Alan hesitated, and Cristan continued, "Sure, you could figure it out with the compass, but what if you get turned around? What if you get a mile away from here and you sit down for a water break. When you stand up, you check the compass to remind yourself which way to go … but you can't quite remember if you were supposed to be going northeast or northwest. You choose one, but it's the wrong one, and you end up wandering off in the wrong direction, never to be seen again."

"That wouldn't happen," Alan scoffed.

"It happens *all the time*," Cristan said.

"I'll write the direction down on a scrap of paper, if you're so worried about it," Alan said.

"What happens if you twist your ankle an hour into the trip? Or you get bit by a snake? What happens if you drop the compass and it hits a rock and breaks? I may not be a hiker like Ricardo, but I've lived out here all my life. The desert kills people every year. People like you, who think it's as easy as choosing a direction and hitting a road eventually. It also kills people like Ricardo, who have been hiking and camping in the area for years. It's stupid to go out there if you don't know what you're doing. I agree with what Noah said last night; staying out here is the smarter choice. We have food and water, shelter, and when a rescue team comes for us, they'll know where to find us."

"What happens if we run out of water?" Alan shot back. "We all have enough for three days, but what if it takes them four days to realize something's wrong? Or five days, or six? Even Ricardo said we might have to end up staying out another night if someone got hurt and we couldn't get back as quickly as we got out here. What if Ricardo's boss thinks that's what happened and doesn't send rescue out right away?"

"We have more than enough food and water as long as we're smart about how we use it," Cristan said, his voice calm. "Remember, we have Ricardo's supplies too. He's not going to need them. We'll divvy them up between us. We should drink when we're thirsty, but conserve water other than that."

Tulia thought about the wasted water when she brushed her teeth and washed her face and winced. She'd be more careful from now on.

The argument must have woken Noah, because he unzipped his tent and stepped out, blinking blearily in the sun. "What's going on?" he asked.

"We're trying to figure out what to do," Alan said. "I already know whose side you're on. He turned to Tulia, and glanced at Rosemary as well. The other woman had been watching them silently, the sour expression back on her face. "What about you two? Will you come with me to look for help?"

Tulia hesitated. "I think I'm going to stay here," she said. "It does seem like the safer option. I think we should wait here until we're getting low on water, and if rescue hasn't come, then maybe we can chance trying to find our own way back."

Alan made a sound of annoyance and turned to Rosemary, who shook her head. "I'm staying. Someone will come find us when we don't show up. A lot of people know I'm out here. I told my friends and family when I'm supposed to be back, and if they can't get in touch with me, they'll know something is wrong. Even if the tour company doesn't send rescue, my sister will."

Scoffing, Alan turned toward his tent. "Well, I'm going. None of you have a right to stop me; it's my choice. I'll tell the police what happened, and they'll send someone out to get you. Buncha' cowards." He muttered the last part, and Tulia saw Cristan's hand tense into a fist, but he let it go.

"He's right, we can't stop him," Cristan said over the sounds of Alan packing his things. "I just hope this turns out better than I think it will."

# CHAPTER SIX

With Alan determined to go, all Tulia could do was watch while he prepared for his solitary trek. He took his own water and food supplies, and Cristan ended up finding the compass Ricardo was using. He let him have it, though he seemed reluctant to do so.

"I'm leaving my tent here," Alan said, hefting his backpack. It seemed less full than before; he must have packed light so he could move more quickly. "It should only take me a couple of hours to get back. My clothes and some other things are in my tent—I'd appreciate it if no one went in there. With any luck, everyone will be rescued by dark."

They said goodbye to him with varying degrees of enthusiasm. Rosemary wished him good luck and gave him a quick hug. The rest of them held back.

Tulia felt anxious—she didn't think it was a good idea for him to leave, but she didn't think more arguing would do anyone any good. He knew the risks, and it was his choice. That would have to be good enough, no matter what ended up happening.

They all stood at the top of the path and watched him make his way down it. At the bottom, he paused to turn around and wave at them, then set out again, not looking back a second time. At last, Rosemary cleared her throat.

"Well, I don't know about you all, but it's going to drive me crazy if I just sit around and wait for him alone. We should do something."

"Like what?" Cristan asked. "There isn't exactly a television out here."

"We could just talk," Rosemary suggested. "Get to know each other. We might be out here for a while."

Noah shrugged. "If you want company, I'll sit with you, but I don't feel like sharing my life story."

They turned and started walking back towards their camp. Tulia shot one last look over her shoulder at Alan, who was still visible in the distance. Then she turned back and quickened her steps to catch up to the others.

"Why are you even out here, anyway?" Rosemary

asked Noah. "You don't seem like you're enjoying any of this. You've been in your tent practically the whole time. And you hardly said a thing to anyone. You didn't even look for aliens last night."

"I looked at the stars," Noah grumbled. "I don't believe in aliens."

"Then why are you on a tour that specifically advertises the possibility of seeing a UFO?" Rosemary pressed.

"My daughter liked this kind of thing, okay?" Noah snapped. "She passed away two years ago. I'm doing this in memory of her. I don't want to talk about it."

He quickened his pace, leaving the rest of them behind, and Rosemary slowed until she was walking next to Tulia.

"I had no idea," she murmured. "I feel really bad now. I shouldn't have said anything."

"Maybe not," Tulia said. "But you couldn't have known. I think we're all on edge after what happened, anyway. We can sit and talk if you want. I don't really want to sit around on my own either."

But they didn't get a chance to sit down, because when they returned to camp, Cristan was on his knees in front of Alan's tent, the door unzipped and his head poking inside. Tulia frowned.

"Hey, what are you doing?" she called out, striding over to him. She wasn't sure she should get involved, but Alan had *just* asked them not to bother his things, and she didn't want to sit back and say nothing either. A quick glance around showed her that Noah wasn't anywhere in sight—he must've already gone back into his own tent. She could understand why Rosemary was wondering why he had even come on this tour, but she couldn't exactly blame him for not wanting to be social given their current situation.

"I'm looking through his things," Cristan said, withdrawing from the tent to look up at her. "Doesn't it seem strange to you, that he asked us not to go in here?"

"I mean, I wouldn't want a bunch of strangers poking through my stuff either," Tulia said. "I know you don't think he should go out into the desert alone, and I agree, but that doesn't change the fact he's trying to do a good thing. He wants to get help for all of us, and the least we can do is not break his confidence the first chance we get."

"Look, we all know someone pushed Ricardo off the edge," Cristan said. "Has it escaped your attention that Alan is doing his best to leave the scene of the crime at the first chance? Maybe trying to find help was an excuse, and he wants to take this chance to hop on a bus to Mexico."

"And, what, you think he left evidence of a murder in his tent?" She didn't mean to sound so skeptical. What he was saying did make some sense, and she didn't know any of these people well enough to vouch for them.

"If he did, I'd rather find out now than later. Plus, I think I found something already."

She watched as he ducked back into the tent and came out a moment later with an old, dusty, ripped canvas bag he dropped on the ground between them. Rosemary, who had been watching from a distance, came over.

"What is that?" she asked, curious.

"I don't know," Cristan said. "Alan was hiding it."

Tulia watched, her arms folded, as Cristan bent down to unzip it. If it was full of socks, she was never going to let him hear the end of it.

But it wasn't full of socks. He unzipped the top and tipped it over, and stack after stack of cash tumbled out.

The three of them stared at the money. Cristan kicked the bag, and more stacks of cash came falling out. "I'd say I told you so, but I have to admit, even I wasn't expecting this."

"Where did all that money come from?" Rosemary asked, her eyes wide. She bent down and picked up a stack of bills. "It's all hundreds."

"I don't know," Cristan said. "But I bet you anything, this much cash is enough motive to get just about anyone to commit murder."

Tulia crouched on the ground next to Rosemary and looked through the stacks of bills. They really were all hundreds, and though she was no expert, they didn't look like fakes either.

"This must have been here for a while," she said, dropping the stack of cash back into the pile. "It's all sandy and dirty. Look at the bag, it's all beat up."

"He must have found it during the hike," Rosemary said, standing up and wiping her hands off on her jean shorts. Tulia thought she saw one of her hands slip into her pocket with one of the stacks of bills, but wasn't sure and didn't say anything. She wasn't sure how many stacks of cash there had been before, and wasn't about to raise the issue when they were all depending on each other alone in the wilderness.

"Maybe Ricardo saw him with it and Alan killed him to keep it quiet," Cristan said.

"I'm kind of surprised he didn't want to stay, or didn't try to take the cash with him," Tulia said.

"Sure, the bag was heavy, but it still seems strange for him to just leave it behind."

"The bag is only about half full," Cristan pointed out. "And if you look in his tent, it looks like most of his supplies except for a little water and probably some food were left behind. I bet you anything he packed as much money into his backpack as he could comfortably carry and took off. I doubt we'll see him again. He must've killed Ricardo, and decided to take his chances and run." Cristan kicked at the bag of money viciously and turned to stalk away. Rosemary looked down at the money, then back up at Tulia.

"So, you're pretty sure it's murder, then?"

"I'm sure I heard him talking to someone just before he fell," Tulia said. "Either someone killed him, or someone saw him slip and is lying about it for some reason. And now, with the money…" She trailed off. She didn't want to lay the blame on Alan, not without getting his side of the story, but it was all beginning to make sense.

"I hope someone figures out we're stuck here soon," Rosemary said. "What if Alan comes back? What if he realizes we found the money? Maybe we should pack it up and put it back in the tent."

That seemed like a better solution than leaving it all lying out there in the open, so Tulia knelt down and helped Rosemary shovel the stacks of cash back into the bag. It was a little strange to feel absolutely no temptation as her fingers brushed across the dusty hundred-dollar bills. She had more money than this in her checking account alone.

As she fought with the rusted zipper, she couldn't help but wonder how much her lottery winnings had changed her. The world she lived in now, though it might not seem like it at first glance, was a completely different one from the one the people around her inhabited. She decided not to say anything about the stack of cash she thought she saw Rosemary slip into her pocket, even after they got back to civilization. It wasn't her business, and besides, who was she to judge? She would have felt like a horrible hypocrite judging Rosemary over a misplaced stack of hundreds when she was sitting on a hoard many times greater than that, one she hadn't really earned either.

## CHAPTER SEVEN

The day passed by in fits and starts, the hot sun beating down on them. Tulia took a nap in her tent and woke up sweating. She gulped her water, and only after did she feel guilt and wonder if she had wasted it. The advice, she knew, was to drink when you were thirsty and not try to conserve water too much, but it still felt indulgent to have drunk so much.

After she stopped feeling so groggy, she left her tent and joined Cristan and Rosemary, who were sitting in the central area of the camp and talking quietly. Rosemary greeted her when she sat down nearby.

"We were just talking about whether or not Alan should have made it back yet," she said. "Cristan thinks he would have, but I think it would take him longer, even if he didn't get lost."

"Maybe another hour," Tulia said. "But it should be soon. The real question is how long it would take a rescue team to get back here. Do you think they would try to get out here tonight?"

"It probably depends on what he tells them," Cristan said. "On the off chance he makes it, it would probably take him a while to get in contact with the right people to help us. If it's dark by the time he does, and he tells them the truth about our supplies—that we have enough for a couple of days —they might not bother mounting a rescue expedition until the morning." Rosemary looked like she was about to complain and he continued, saying, "And I wouldn't blame them. We aren't in any immediate danger. None of us are hurt or sick, we have food and water, we have shelter. It wouldn't make sense to put a rescue team at risk when they could just let us wait for a few hours and come during the daylight."

Rosemary gave an exaggerated sigh. "I know you're right. I hate it, but I know you are. I just hate not knowing. I wish we had phone service out here. Why don't they just put more cell towers up?"

"There are a lot of restrictions out here. This is all

protected land," he said. "Plus, it's usually nice to get away for a while. This is an unusual situation."

They chatted for a while longer, and gradually, the sun began to set. Noah stepped out of his tent and went off into the distance to relieve himself. When he rejoined their group, Cristan got up and started gathering branches.

"What are you doing?" Rosemary asked. "I thought we couldn't have fires out here."

"It's illegal, sure, but it's not windy right now. There is no real danger of a wildfire starting. I'll dig a pit just to be safe, but it'll be nice to have some warmth once the sun goes down. Maybe we can even cook some food over it. Plus, if someone sees the smoke or the flames, they may come investigate."

"That's a great idea," Tulia said, getting up to help him gather some burnable materials. "I wish we had thought about it earlier."

Using a few rocks and sticks, they dug a fire pit, and lit a small fire using a lighter Noah had in his backpack. With the sun falling and a cheerful little blaze going, it was almost cozy, or it would have been if Tulia wasn't keenly aware that there was a dead man wrapped in a blanket at the bottom of the plateau.

They ate a light dinner, none of them seeming to

have much of an appetite. It felt strange to just sit in silence without a phone to scroll through or the TV on in the background, but even though she wasn't currently engaged with anything, Tulia wasn't bored either. It was almost relaxing.

At least, until they heard the sound of a rock falling down the steep slope of the plateau. They all turned to look toward the path where Alan had gone down hours before.

"Hello?" Cristan called out, standing up. Tulia felt her heart begin to beat harder. She was suddenly keenly aware that they were miles and miles from any civilization. They had been hoping to attract attention and get rescued with the smoke, but what if they had attracted someone else? Someone who would take advantage of a group of defenseless people?

They all tensed as they heard more footsteps, and then Alan's head poked over the ridge. Tulia slumped, both relieved and disappointed. Part of her had been hoping she'd see someone official who had come to save them.

"Thank goodness," Alan gasped. He looked much the worse for wear, sunburned and covered in sweat. One of his pant legs was ripped, and he walked with a slight limp as he hurried over to the fire, dropping his bag at his feet before collapsing onto a flat rock. "Does anyone have water?"

Rosemary got up to fetch him some, and he guzzled it down, then splashed the remainder over his face. Tulia winced, but didn't say anything. They waited until he was looking a little better before Noah finally asked, "What happened?"

"I got lost," Alan admitted without a trace of embarrassment. "Just like you said." He nodded at Cristan. "I kept getting turned around, and I was trying to look at the compass while I walked, and I ended up stumbling and twisting my ankle. I had no way to track how many miles I'd covered. And the compass stopped working—I think it brushed against the magnet I have in my bill clip. It was acting all weird, and kept spinning around. I thought for sure I was going to die out there, then I saw the smoke from this fire. You guys saved my life."

"I'm glad you were able to find your way back," Cristan said, clasping him on the shoulder. "We'll get you some food. We'll start rationing, but we'll only have to hold out here for another day or two at the most. We'll be just fine."

After darkness fell, they let the fire die down. It was chilly, but there wasn't much to burn on the plateau, and the fire had been burning for long enough that if someone was going to see it, they would have. She doubted there were that many people out there in the desert so late at night.

It was late, but Tulia was not tired. Maybe it was due to the relief of the sun finally setting and the cooler night air coming in, or thanks to the nap she had taken earlier that day, but she was content to just lay out under the stars instead of crawling into her tent. Rosemary set up near her, and they stargazed together, pointing out the various constellations they knew. Tulia had been making a point of learning more constellations recently, and was proud that she was able to point them out to the other woman. Suddenly, Rosemary gasped.

"Look! That is not a shooting star."

Tulia turned, fully expecting to see another airplane, but what she saw instead chilled her to her core. A formation of lights was moving in the distance over the desert. It grew and shrank, making forms no regular aircraft could do as it rose, fell, turned, twisted, and spun across the night sky. Rosemary shouted for the others, and they rushed out of their tents to see. Alan was just as awed as the two of them were, but Noah only glanced at the lights before shaking his head and stomping back into seclusion.

Cristan watched silently until the lights vanished, one by one, then started chuckling.

"What is it?" Rosemary asked. "What's so funny? There is no way that was an airplane or a shooting star."

Cristan just shook his head. "It was quite the show," he said cryptically. "I'm glad you guys got a chance to see it. I'm heading to bed. With any luck, we'll be out of here tomorrow."

## CHAPTER EIGHT

Tulia awoke that morning to the sound of someone shouting outside her tent. "Hey! Get up!"

Groggily, she rubbed her eyes and sat up. She was sleeping in a pair of shorts, since her pajama pants were still all ripped and dusty from the night before, and a T-shirt. The morning was chilly, so she pulled a sweatshirt on before slipping her feet into shoes and crawling out of the tent. Cristan was standing in the center of the clearing, his arms crossed over his chest. Rosemary was standing nearby looking just as sleepy as Tulia felt, and Noah was standing near his tent, watching Cristan.

"What is it? It's the crack of dawn."

"Alan is missing," Cristan said without preamble. "And he took the rest of the money with him."

Tulia blinked and turned back toward Alan's tent. The door was unzipped. She walked over to it, hearing the sound of the others doing the same behind her, and looked in. Sure enough, Alan was gone and so was the dusty old bag that contained all the money.

"This doesn't make any sense," she said, pulling out of the tent to let the others see. "He was in really rough shape yesterday. It sounds like he thought he might not even make it back. Why would he go out again, and in the middle of the night?"

"People leave all common sense behind when money is involved," Noah said, shrugging. "I say if he wants to take off with the money, let him. It's no skin off my back either way. I just want to get out of here without anyone else getting hurt."

"I think we should let him go too," Rosemary chimed in. "Yeah, it's a lot of money, but it's not like he stole it from any of us. Finders keepers, right? It's a lot more important to focus on how we're going to get out of here, isn't it?"

"What do you think?" Cristan asked, looking at Tulia. "If you think we should go look for him, I'm with you, but if you think we should drop it too, I will. I don't like it, but the others have a point. We do have more important things to focus on."

Tulia bit her lip. While she had decided not to say

anything about the money she thought she'd seen Rosemary slip into her pocket, she wasn't actually *sure* she'd seen anything, and that had been one stack of money. Wherever this money had come from, chances were it had been in some way involved in a crime. With the whole bag missing, it could impede the investigation. Even if it was from a decades-old crime, it was still important that it was solved.

But the alternative was trying to track a man through the desert when they were already in danger of running out of food and water and they didn't even have a compass, assuming Alan had taken it. They would use a lot more water and food if they were up and active, she knew, and chances were high that one of them would get lost or hurt.

"I think it's best to let it go," she said with a sigh. "I don't think it's right what he did—I'm sure that money is evidence of *something*. I doubt whoever hid it out here had it legally. But I think keeping everyone safe is more important than tracking down the money. We'll tell the police about it once we're somewhere safe, but until then, we should be focused on our own survival."

"Fine," Cristan said tersely, sounding irritated but unsurprised. "We're letting it go, I guess. But if Alan shows his face again, you'd better believe I'm going to get after him about it. He's not welcome here, as far as I'm concerned, not after this."

He turned toward camp, but then hesitated and turned back around. "What's this?"

Tulia saw him lift a backpack from the ground next to Alan's tent. It was Alan's backpack, she recognized it from the day before. She'd passed right by it just moments ago, but hadn't really registered it, too concerned with confirming that both Alan and the money were gone. Now, she felt an icy chill sweep over her as she realized what the backpack being left behind meant.

"He didn't bring his backpack?" Noah asked, sounding interested for the first time. "That doesn't make any sense."

Cristan crouched down and unzipped the bag. "His water and food is still in here too. And look, the compass."

"Why would he try to get back home without his survival supplies?" Noah asked. "Did he take someone else's? Everyone, you should check your things."

Tulia hurried back to her tent, but she already knew her backpack was in there. She had been using it as a pillow. There was no way he would have been able to sneak it out without her noticing. The rest of them confirmed that their backpacks were all there, and none of them were missing water or food.

"There is no way he would have left without his supplies. He might be reckless by my standards, but he wasn't a complete idiot. Something else must have happened to him." Cristan stood up. "I changed my mind. I think we should go look for him."

Tulia agreed. "If he just took the money and ran, that's one thing, but if he is hurt or lost, we have to find him. No matter what we think he might've done, and we don't actually know for sure he was involved in Ricardo's death, we can't risk leaving him alone and injured somewhere. I'm with you. I'll help you look for him."

Noah and Rosemary both agreed as well, though neither of them sounded enthusiastic about the prospect. It took them another fifteen minutes to get fully dressed and for everyone to get ready for what might be a long trek. They loaded up with water, the first aid kit, and some food, along with the broken compass just in case they could find some use for it, and set out, keeping a few feet apart from each other and scrutinizing the ground carefully. Cristan was the one who found the first footprint at the base of the plateau. It appeared that Alan had been going around the plateau toward where Ricardo's body was.

They found him there, only a few feet away from Ricardo. Thankfully, the body was still securely wrapped in the blanket. Alan, on the other hand, was fully exposed to the sun. He only responded in mumbles when Cristan called out his name, and nearly fell over when he tried to sit up. There was a matted, bloody wound at the back of his head.

"What happened?" she asked as Cristan steadied him and she crouched next to him, pulling the first aid kit out of her backpack. She got out some antibacterial ointment and a gauze pad, and gently dabbed at his wound. He flinched away from her. Noah helped Cristan hold him still while Tulia tended to him and Rosemary hovered awkwardly over her shoulder.

"Someone hit me," Allen mumbled. "Came up behind me. Don't know who. Hit me with a rock, I think."

When she had the gauze pad taped to his head wound, she looked around until she found a large rock with a small red smear on it not far from him. She called the others over. Cristan paused long enough to make sure Alan was comfortable in the shade of a bush and handed him a bottle of water, then joined them.

"Someone attacked him," Noah said in a low voice, carefully looking at the bloody rock without touching it. "One of us, unless there's someone else out here we don't know about."

Tulia fought back a shiver. The idea that one of them had attacked Alan, or the thought that there might be another person out there, one they weren't aware of, filled her with fear, and she didn't know which was worse. Someone might be watching them from afar, even now.

"We've got to get him back up to camp," Cristan said. "He's hurt, but I think he'll be all right if we get help soon. At least he's aware and conscious."

He and Noah went over to Alan to help him up, but Tulia paused, looking around. "Hold on," she said. "The money. Where's the bag with the money?"

The others stilled, looking over at her. Rosemary pressed a hand to her lips. "It's gone," she said, glancing around. "Maybe he hid it."

"Maybe whoever attacked Alan made off with it," Cristan said. With Noah's help, he got Alan to his feet. "Let's go," he grunted. "First things first, we've got to get him back to camp. Then, we'll figure out what to do about the missing money."

# CHAPTER NINE

"He's not doing well."

Tulia was sitting on one of the flat rocks in the middle of their camp, idly tossing pebbles at the dusty ground. It was sweltering hot in the tents, so they had used some long sticks, a tentpole, and a light blanket to make a shaded area for Alan to lie in. Tulia had folded up her own sleeping bag for him to use as a pillow, and Cristan was currently crouched next to him, trying to get him to drink more water.

She looked over to Noah, who had spoken. Rosemary, who was sitting across from her and Noah, spoke up before Tulia could reply. "You don't think he's going to die, do you?"

"I don't know," Noah said, frowning. Tulia followed his gaze and watched as Cristan tried and failed to get Alan to drink. "If anything, I think he's getting worse."

It had only been about an hour since they got Alan up to the top of the plateau. He'd been in and out of consciousness that entire time, and hadn't been able to give them any more answers as to what had happened.

"Is there anything else we can do for him?" Tulia asked. She wished she had phone service here; she itched to search for ways to help someone with a head injury. Of course, if they did have phone service, they would have called an ambulance an hour ago. In a desperate hope that one of them would be able to get even a single bar out here, they had all turned their phones on and walked around the plateau, but to no avail. She was worried about Cicero too; the vet's office thought she was only going to be gone for two nights. She hoped he was doing okay and wasn't too scared.

"The only thing I know about brain injuries is you're not supposed to move someone with a head or neck injury," Noah said. "And we've already broken that rule. If all the medical shows I've seen are right, the real risk is in the swelling of his brain. And there's nothing we can do for that. He needs a hospital."

"Someone should come looking for us soon," Rosemary said. "He just has to hold on until then."

Giving up, Cristan set the water bottle down next to Alan and walked over to them. "He won't drink," he said. "And that's a real concern. Even though he's in the shade, he's still getting dehydrated because the air is so dry. We need to get him somewhere where he can get professional help."

"We were just talking about that," Noah said. "But there's nothing we can do. We can hardly carry him out."

"Maybe we should try," Cristan said, surprising Tulia. "I thought we should wait before, but we are already beginning to run low on water. None of us have done well at rationing it. I'm not blaming anyone, I'm guilty too. I used some to wash my face just a couple hours ago without even thinking about it. But if we run out of water out here, we're out of luck. At this point, I'm thinking it might be better to try to start making our way back. Alan was right in that we do know the general direction to head. With any luck, we will run into a rescue team on the way out.

"What about Alan, though?" Tulia asked. "We can't just leave him here."

"We'll build a stretcher for him," Cristan said. He

must have seen their skeptical expressions, because he crossed his arms. "Look, we have blankets, a pocketknife, and I know Ricardo had some paracord in his bag. We'll find some sturdy branches or tree limbs, cut them to a manageable length, stretch a blanket between them, tie everything together, and load him up on that. There's four of us left. We can take turns teaming up to carry him. Even if we only go half a mile at a time, we will still make some progress."

"And if we get lost?" Noah asked, raising an eyebrow. "I don't see how this plan is any better than Alan's plan was."

"It's not," Cristan said. "But the simple fact of the matter is, we are running out of options. We'll be out of water by tomorrow morning. And that's if something disastrous doesn't happen, like someone accidentally knocking over one of the bottles. Maybe a rescue team is on the way, but maybe not. Our situation has changed, especially with Alan's injury. I think it's best we try to head back." He hesitated. "And I also can't ignore the fact that someone here did this to him. At this point, I don't think it's safe for any of us to be out here. We don't know who's behind this, or who is behind what happened to Ricardo. Do you really want to spend another night out here, not knowing if there is a killer sleeping just a few feet away from you? Ricardo's death could have been an accident, but what happened to Alan wasn't."

His words sent a shiver up Tulia's spine, and it seemed to work on the others too. Rosemary said, "All right, I think I am on your side with this. We should get going. Maybe we should leave a note on the plateau in case the rescue people come here?"

"Good idea," Cristan said. "Everyone should wear their brightest clothing. That way if someone is out there looking for us, or they send a helicopter over, they will be able to see us more easily. We'll have to leave Ricardo where he is, but the authorities can bring him in. I hate it, but we can't carry him out as well as Alan." He ran a hand through his hair, took one last look around the plateau, then said, "Well, let's get to it."

That seemed to settle it. Tulia wasn't sure if leaving was the best idea; she could just imagine them wandering through the desert in the wrong direction, lost and sweltering under the sun, but she also didn't know if staying here was any better. Alan seemed to be getting worse and worse, and she couldn't stomach the thought of staying out here and watching him die. It was worth the risk, she thought as she got up to begin packing her things, if they managed to save him.

She got everything packed back into her backpack and took her tent down. She really was running low on water. They had brought enough for an extra day, but she'd used a lot more than she expected. Her backpack was lighter, but she wished that wasn't the case as she shouldered it. She would much rather have to carry a few extra pounds and know she had the extra water to go along with it.

She was one of the first ones done. Rosemary was still in her tent, and Cristan hadn't even started packing since he was busy trying to make the stretcher for Alan. Noah was done, though, so she went to sit by him on the rocks, carefully reapplying her sunscreen. She was trying to gear herself up for the upcoming hike. After doing so much sitting around, at least her muscles were in better shape, but it was going to be hard to want to keep going when she knew chances were good they were just going to end up lost.

"This is a bad situation," Noah muttered. She turned to look at him, curious despite herself.

"Is this the first time you've done anything like this?" she asked.

"The hike?" he asked. "It is. I've never seen the appeal of exercising in the heat when I can get the same results in an air-conditioned gym. My daughter, though, she was always into it. Her mother and I divorced when she was younger, and I only saw her on weekends, and then even less often once she was older, but she would always tell me about her latest great adventure when we got together." He gave a sad smile. "I can see why she liked it, almost. If she was here now, though, I'd say I told you so. I always told her going out here like this was dangerous. I just wish she had listened."

"If you don't mind me asking," she said. "Your daughter… How old was she?"

"She was twenty-two," he said, closing his eyes for a moment as if in remembrance. "She'd be twenty-four now. It was a tour like this, almost the exact same situation in fact, except they were in a rockier area, and she was with a bigger group. She went off the path for some reason, slipped, fell off a rock, and hit her head. It must have knocked her out, because she didn't call for help. The tour guide didn't notice until the group was almost back that she was missing. The rescue team didn't get out until the next day, and by then, she had already passed away."

His story made Tulia wish she'd never brought it up, both because of the grief it caused him, and because it was so close to their own situation. "I'm so sorry. That should have never happened. I can't even imagine what you went through."

"So many people in my life keep telling me it was an accident, that she died doing something she loved, as if that makes it better," he said, his voice bitter. "The tour company dissolved, but no one faced any charges. My daughter died because the man in charge of her safety wasn't paying attention. The fact that she was doing something she loved doesn't make it any better. If she'd lived, she would have had a lifetime to do the things she loved." He shook his head. "Sorry. I don't think it will ever stop hurting. But I shouldn't be talking about this right now. We've got our own mess to get out of." He looked over to Alan. "I couldn't do anything to help my daughter, but that man over there, he's someone else's son. He might be older than she was, but that doesn't mean he doesn't have parents who love him. I'm going to do everything I can to make sure they don't have to go through the same pain I did."

# CHAPTER TEN

The makeshift stretcher—a blanket with a sturdy limb on each end so two people could carry it—worked when they tested it, with Tulia as the volunteer. It wasn't the most comfortable ride, but it was more comfortable than hiking would be after a few hours, and Alan didn't seem coherent enough to really notice, anyway.

Cristan and Noah carried him on the stretcher down from the plateau, with the two women spotting on either side of them. When they reached the bottom they took a short break, made sure Alan didn't seem to be doing any worse with all the jostling, and then picked up the stretcher again, this time with Tulia at the feet and Noah at the head. They had decided to take turns with one man and one woman carrying him at a time. Since both men had more significant upper body strength it made sense to split it this way, with the men carrying the front half of the stretcher where more of Alan's body weight was, and the woman carrying the back half. After even just a few hundred yards, Tulia's hands began to ache, and eyeing the makeshift stretcher, she had an idea.

"Why don't all four of us carry it?" she suggested. "There's enough space, and it will be easier going that way."

"Like pallbearers?" Rosemary asked. Tulia winced at the comparison, but nodded.

They tried it that way, and it worked better than having one person in front and one behind. At least Tulia's muscles weren't aching by the time they decided to take a break.

They sat for fifteen minutes, sipped their water, then started moving again. They traveled this way for hours before finding a low rock formation that offered them some scant shade. Tulia reapplied her sunscreen and leaned against the rocks, wishing she was back in her RV with the air-conditioning on.

Cristan and the others sat nearby. They were all silent for a while, drinking the water, with Tulia looking at the wide blue sky. It was so empty out here. She didn't even see any birds wheeling in the air above them.

The thought of something in the sky reminded her of what she had seen the other night.

"Cristan?" she said, getting his attention. "What were those lights in the sky? You laughed at them, and I got the feeling you knew what they were."

He flushed. "I promised not to say anything, but I guess it doesn't matter now. Ricardo hired some guys to fly their drones on the second night of the tour. They have some program that links them all together so they can do synchronized formations. His boss doesn't know about it, but he's done it a few times. He likes to give people a thrill."

"So there were people out there flying drones?" Tulia asked. Her heart began to beat faster. "They couldn't have been far away. Half a mile, a mile at most. If you had said something, we could've followed the lights and found them. I bet they had vehicles out there, or at least nearby. We could be back in town by now."

His flush darkened, and he tossed a stone away, watching it bounce in the dry dirt. "I didn't think of it. I'm such an idiot. We could have been rescued by now."

"If he dies out here, it's your fault," Noah said

darkly, nodding at Alan, who shifted slightly, mumbling incoherently. Rosemary gingerly tried to dribble some water into his mouth, shooting Cristan a glare.

"I really thought they were aliens," she admitted. "I thought well, even if I die out here, at least I know we're not alone in the universe. So, thanks for that, Cristan. Not only is it your fault if we die out here, but it's also your fault I'll die disappointed."

None of them talked much after that. The sun was at its zenith, and they moved to shade Alan better. They put it to a vote and decided to sit tight for at least another hour, until the sun started to go down a bit and its rays were less direct.

While they relaxed, Tulia took her phone out to see if they had any service yet. Still nothing, and she was beginning to feel anxious about not being able to talk to Samuel about Luis or check in on Cicero. She was more than ready to get back to her regular life.

She set a timer for an hour to remind them to get going and leaned her head back against the rock, draping a shirt over her eyes. It was too hot to fall asleep, but she still was able to doze until her phone beeped to alert her it was time to go.

"What is that?" Rosemary asked, sitting up like a shot to her left. "Are you getting phone service?"

"No, I set an alarm," Tulia said apologetically, turning it off. "I didn't want to risk us all falling asleep or something. We have to be back before dark, or else we'll have to camp out again."

"It's still so hot out though," Rosemary complained. "Aren't we getting toward the hottest part of the day? The sun might be starting to go down a little bit, but I always heard late afternoon was the worst for heat."

"We don't have much of a choice," Cristan said. "We've got to get out of here. Drink your water, then pack up, everyone. Let's get going."

Tulia drank her water, which was getting perilously low. She drank as much as she dared and then tucked the rest back into her bag before standing up and stretching.

They checked on Alan and made sure the stretcher was still secure, and all got to the proper positions to pick it up. They took a step in the direction Tulia thought they were supposed to go, but Noah paused, squinting in the sun.

"Weren't we supposed to be heading east?" he asked.

"Yeah," Cristan said. "We went roughly northwest from the parking lot to the plateau. East, southeast— as long as we hit the road, we will probably be okay.

It's a relatively busy area, and we can flag someone down to ask for help."

"Well, the sun is beginning to go down, right? It's afternoon. So we should be heading away from it. It should be at our backs, not to our side."

"I don't think so," Tulia said. "We weren't hiking directly toward it when we first set out toward the plateau, so we shouldn't be heading directly away from it."

"I think we're heading the wrong way," Noah insisted. "We should go more to the right."

"I think it's better just to go the way we've been going. We know the road runs north and south. We will hit it at some point."

"That could add miles to our trip," Noah said. "We should be trying to take the most direct route."

"I don't know what the right answer is, but either way, we should just keep moving," Tulia said. "Let's adjust our course a little, and start walking. We're not going anywhere if we stand here and argue."

That got them moving at least, though the men kept arguing. Rosemary looked too tired and hot to say anything, and Tulia was with her. Maybe leaving the plateau hadn't been such a good idea, after all.

They walked for hours until the sun started touching the horizon, but there was still no road in sight. They were almost out of water. Tulia had maybe the equivalent of another water bottle left. They still had most of Alan's water, since he wasn't drinking much, but it wouldn't last them long split between the group.

"I can't go anymore," Rosemary said at last, stopping. They carefully put Alan's stretcher down. Thankfully, the sun wasn't beating down on them anymore, but he still seemed out of it. He had woken up briefly to ask for water, but that was it.

"I think we're lost," Noah admitted. "We're going to die out here."

He didn't say it like he was afraid; his voice was grim and resigned. She remembered what had happened to his daughter and wondered if he thought it was some sort of poetic alignment of the stars, him dying in a similar manner to how his daughter had.

"Maybe we should set up camp," Cristan relented. "Things might look better in the morning. We should try lighting a fire again, too, in case a rescue team is out looking for us."

Tulia was hot, thirsty, and uncomfortable. She wanted a shower and an ice-cold soda, not another uncomfortable evening by a campfire, but there was no alternative. They got Alan comfortable and set up their tents, then Cristan built a fire while Tulia did her best to tidy herself up without the use of any water, which mostly involved brushing her hair and brushing her teeth, trying to spit out the toothpaste without rinsing. With her hair in a fresh ponytail and her teeth somewhat clean, if overly minty, she felt the slightest bit better. She was thirsty but didn't want to drink more water. She knew she'd be even worse off in the morning if she finished it tonight. She would drink the rest of it right before they set out the next day.

The four of them took turns getting up to scavenge for dry brush to throw on the fire. They kept it going as long as they could, but night fell, and they didn't see any lights out in the dark, flat expanse of the desert.

With a sinking feeling, Tulia realized no one was out there looking for them.

They went to bed as soon as the fire was out, none of them bothering to bid the others good night.

# CHAPTER ELEVEN

Tulia hadn't done a good job of clearing the space where her tent was of rocks, and spent the first part of the night shifting around, struggling to get comfortable. She finally dozed off to the sound of Alan mumbling in his sleep. He was as comfortable as they could make him, but the only painkillers any of them had were aspirin, and both Tulia and Noah remembered hearing that you weren't supposed to give someone with a brain injury aspirin because it could thin the blood and cause a stroke.

She woke up sometime later to the sound of a tent unzipping. She lay there in the quiet, hearing various calls of desert animals and the sound of someone moving around outside of their tent. She figured one of the others was going to check on Alan, and waited to hear their response, assuming they would wake the others if he had passed in his sleep.

But all she heard was footsteps, going away. She sat up, listening as the steps faded away into the distance. If someone needed to duck behind a bush, they were sure going quite a ways away to do it.

Curious, she unzipped her own tent as quietly as possible, slipped her shoes on, grabbed her lantern, though she left it off for the time being, and stepped out of the tent. She saw right away that Rosemary's tent was the one that was open. She paused near the entrance, ducking down to look inside, though of course Rosemary wasn't there. The woman was gone … but so was her backpack. Frowning, Tulia straightened up and looked around. It was dark out, but the stars were bright, and she could see a person's silhouette a few hundred feet away against the horizon line. Rosemary was walking steadily farther away from camp, heading east, if her position relative to that of the setting moon was any indication.

Tulia set off after her, curious. Had Rosemary seen lights in the distance? It wasn't impossible that they would be able to see lights of people driving on the road far off in the distance now that it was so dark out. She couldn't imagine why else the other woman would leave in the middle of the night.

She quickened her pace, wanting to catch up to the other woman. When she was a good distance away from camp, she called out, keeping her voice low and hoping it carried enough that Rosemary would hear it.

"Rosemary, wait."

The figure ahead of her halted. Tulia hurried to catch up. Rosemary turned slowly, her face just visible in the starlight. Tulia was tempted to turn on her lantern, but she knew the light would obliterate their night vision. If something *was* out there, she wanted to be able to see it.

"Did you see something? More lights?" Tulia asked, hopeful.

Rosemary hesitated, then nodded.

"I thought I saw something. I was going to see if I could go find it. You can go back to bed. I don't think I'll be gone very long. I was probably just imagining it, but if someone is out there, looking for us…"

"Yeah, we can't take the chance that someone is passing us by. Do you want me to go with you? Or maybe I should wait here with the lantern on, so you can find your way back if it turns out to be nothing. I could start another fire, maybe?"

The other woman shook her head. "Don't worry.

Like I said, I'm not going far. You can go back to bed."

Tulia hesitated. Something about Rosemary's reaction was giving her pause. Why was the other woman so resistant to her helping? If Tulia thought she found lights, she knew she would want to do everything in her power to make sure the others were aware and that she didn't get lost in the process of trying to find help.

"Really, I'd rather help you. I don't want you to get lost. It's dark out there, and you shouldn't go alone."

"I said I'm fine," Rosemary said, sounding annoyed. "You should go back to camp, Tulia."

"No," Tulia said, crossing her arms, the lantern bumping against her side. "I don't think I will."

Their voices must have carried because Cristan called out from camp, "What are the two of you doing? Go to bed."

"See? Go back to bed," Rosemary said. "Everything will be fine, Tulia. I don't need your help."

Tulia hesitated. Finally, she sighed. "All right. Just … be careful. I don't want anyone else to get hurt. I want us all to make it back safely, okay?"

Rosemary seemed to soften. "I know," she said. "And we will. Don't worry about me. Go back to sleep, all right? The sun won't be up for another few hours."

Tulia still didn't like it, but what could she do? She wasn't about to wrestle Rosemary down and force her to stay, and she also wasn't sure she wanted to follow the woman into the midnight desert without any other explanation. That would just end up with them both lost.

Finally, she gave the other woman another muttered, "Be careful," then turned to go back to camp. She heard Rosemary continue walking behind her, and then the sound of the woman stumbling. Tulia turned around just as Rosemary fell, a rock rolling under her foot. She hit the ground hard on her side, and when she got up, her backpack was dangling from her shoulder by one strap. She let it fall to the ground and rubbed her elbow.

Tulia hurried over, turning the lantern on and setting it next to the offending rock. She could already see that Rosemary's elbow was scraped pretty badly, and the other woman gave a quiet, "Ow," as Tulia looked at it.

"That looks pretty bad. At least put some ointment on it before you go."

"I think I need to borrow someone's backpack

too," Rosemary said, looking down at her own. "The strap broke on mine."

Tulia looked down at it too and saw that the strap had separated from the bag, leaving a rip in the fabric. She crouched down, wondering if it could be fixed somehow, and saw something through the rip that made her frown. It was dirty, torn canvas.

"What's—" she started, reaching for it, but Rosemary snatched the backpack away.

"It's nothing, don't worry about it," she said. "Look, I'll be fine. Just leave me be."

Tulia straightened up slowly, grabbing her lantern. "That was the bag the money was in," she said. She eyed the overstuffed backpack, Rosemary's furtive expression, and felt her stomach drop as she realized what it meant for the other woman to have it.

## CHAPTER TWELVE

"You're the one who attacked Alan."

Rosemary took a step back. "No, I—I—"

"Don't try to lie," Tulia told her, feeling bitter and betrayed. "I know you stole one stack of the bills. I wasn't going to say anything. But you wanted more, didn't you? You must've seen him leaving camp with the money, and you followed him."

"You have no proof. I just found the bag—"

"What's going on here?" It was Cristan, who had come up behind Tulia and looked annoyed. He was holding up another lantern, glaring sleepily at the two of them. "What are you arguing about? It's the middle of the night."

"Remember how the money Alan found went missing after we found him injured?" Tulia asked, crossing her arms. "Rosemary has it in her backpack. And she was trying to sneak away from camp with it."

Cristan raised his lantern to look at Rosemary, who had her arms crossed. Then he looked at the backpack on the ground, which had split further. His expression hardened.

"I see." He bent down to pick the backpack up. Rosemary moved as if to grab it but held herself back at the last moment. "One of our group is dead, the other might not even make it until morning, and the rest of us might die of dehydration before we see another person. Your first thought is to make off into the desert with some cash." He stared Rosemary down. "I'm going back to camp, but you're not welcome. You can die out here in the desert for all I care; that's what you were leaving us to do, so it's fair."

With that, he turned and walked away, the backpack in hand. Rosemary started crying, quiet sobs that she tried to hide. Tulia hesitated, then said, "I agree with him, with everything he said... Except for leaving you out here. Tell me the truth about what happened to Alan."

Between sobs, Rosemary said, "I did attack him. I'm so sorry. I wish I could undo it. I saw him sneaking out of camp with the bag of cash, and I followed. When I found him, he was pacing out a few steps from that tree on the hill Ricardo's body was under. I watched as he started digging a hole. I think he must've been planning on hiding the money and coming back after we were rescued to get it. I just… I wanted it for myself. The money from the lawsuit is enough to keep me going for a few months but not much longer. I've *loved* not working. I don't want to go back to that. It was hell. This money would keep me going for years. I barely even thought before I did it. I snuck up and hit him with the rock, and when he collapsed, I took the bag. I—I thought he was dead. I was lying awake in my tent afterward, all night long, wondering how I could have done that. I know it was wrong. And then, seeing him hurt…" She shook her head. "But I can't go back and redo it. I thought my best chance to avoid being searched when we find civilization and tell the police everything would be to just vanish. I figured I could find the road on my own from here. I'm sorry. I know what I did was wrong. I know I shouldn't have done it. Can you ever forgive me?"

"This isn't a matter of forgiving you, it's a matter of not wanting anyone else to die out here." Tulia took a deep breath. "Come back to camp. I'll defend you. But you've got to just sit in your tent. Don't cause any more trouble. Don't try to take the money back. I think I can convince them to let you stay tonight, but if you try anything else, I won't be able to."

"Thank you," Rosemary said. Tulia shrank back when the woman tried to hug her. They returned to camp, Tulia keeping a good few feet between them. Cristan was still up and gave them a nasty look.

"Didn't I say I don't want her in camp?"

"It's not your camp," Tulia pointed out. "I don't support what she did at all, and I'm certainly going to tell the police about it, but I also don't think we should leave her out here to die. We'll keep an eye on her, and hope we find our way back tomorrow. The police can handle it from there."

"I'm not sleeping," Cristan said, dropping down onto the ground to sit. He had Rosemary's pink backpack next to him. "Not with her around."

"I'll help you keep watch," Tulia said. She turned toward her tent to get her sleeping bag so she would have a way to keep warm. As she passed by, Noah came out of his own tent.

"What's going on out here? Did you three see something?"

"Go ask Rosemary," Tulia muttered, still feeling sour and sad about the whole thing.

When Tulia left her tent with her sleeping bag, Rosemary was telling him and Cristan, who was listening in with curiosity despite himself, the whole story. There were two lanterns on, giving the campsite an eerie glow.

When she finished the story, Noah shook his head, sitting down across from Cristan. "I'm with Tulia. We'll help you get out of the desert, but you're not getting away with this. Alan still might die. You've got to answer for what you did."

"Are you all ignoring the elephant in the room, or do you really not see it?" Cristan asked.

"What are you talking about?" Tulia asked tiredly, sitting down with her back against a rock. She draped her sleeping bag over her legs. She wanted some water but didn't want to break down and finish it yet.

"She killed Ricardo," Cristan said, pointing an accusing finger at Rosemary. "She killed my friend. You're just letting her sit there, and doing nothing about it."

Tulia felt a chill. Nothing alleviated the way she felt about Ricardo's death. Even though it was so recent, felt like it had happened long ago. Everything about Alan felt more immediate, since he was still alive and they had been so focused on getting him help. But now, she realized she had been overlooking the link between them. She turned slowly to Rosemary, who held up her hands.

"I swear, I didn't—"

"Don't," Tulia said tiredly. "He saw you with the money, didn't he? You're who he was arguing with. You pushed him off the cliff, didn't you?"

"No, I swear I didn't," she said, raising her hands. "I swear—"

Rosemary broke off, giving a soft yelp as she looked at something behind Tulia, who turned to see Cristan pointing his gun at the other woman. Noah half stood, looking concerned.

"Tell the truth," Cristan said coldly. "Enough with the lies. You killed my friend. Admit it."

"I didn't do it. I *swear*. I'm not lying." Her voice was full of panicked urgency.

Cristan pulled back the hammer. Rosemary screamed. Noah stood up, moving in front of her and holding his hands out in a gesture to Cristan to stop.

"Enough," he said. "I did it."

That silenced all of them. Cristan let the hand with the gun drop to his side. "What? You're lying. Trying to protect her."

"I'm not," Noah said. "I killed him. That's why I came out here on this hike. I was here to kill him."

"You wanted to kill him? Why?" Cristan asked, sounding stunned.

Noah clenched his jaw and looked away, and Tulia realized with a sneaking feeling that he had told her already, though in a sideways sort of way.

"Your daughter, right?" she said gently. "You said the tour guide who was in charge was still working. The company dissolved, but the man in charge of the tour didn't get punished. That man was Ricardo, wasn't it?"

Noah nodded slowly, still looking away. "It was Ricardo. He is the reason my daughter died. Nothing happened. He didn't get charged with anything, he didn't get fined. The worst thing he had to deal with was finding a new job. When I found out he had started working for a new tour company, I decided to take matters into my own hands. I came out here planning to kill him." Finally, he turned to meet their eyes. "I know you think what I did was wrong. Maybe it was, I don't know. All I know was I couldn't let my little girl's death go unaccounted for. I don't regret what I did." He met Cristan's eyes. "But I don't want anyone else to die. I don't want any other parent to go through what I went through when I found out my daughter was dead. I might have killed a man, but I'm not a bad guy. And I don't want anyone else to get hurt."

For a moment, Tulia was afraid that Cristan was going to raise the gun again, but all of the air seemed to have gone out of him. Rosemary was crying quietly, but Tulia just sat there, shocked. Behind them, Alan groaned and mumbled something. Noah slumped and walked away from Rosemary to sit down on the ground. He didn't say another word. None of them did until morning. With the first light of dawn came a helicopter, and Tulia and Cristan were the only ones with enough energy left to get up, find their signal mirrors and some bright clothing, and start waving the helicopter over.

Rescue had come, but the atmosphere in camp had never been less cheerful.

# EPILOGUE

*I have no idea what's going to happen to the money, but if I ever hear anything about it, you guys will be the first to know. Alan found it that first night, on the plateau, after everyone else went to bed. No one's come forward to claim it yet, but hopefully someone will share something soon.*

Tulia finished writing the blog post, proofread it, and hit the button to post it. It felt good to post again; she missed being able to update her followers as things went along. It was just one more freedom Luis had taken from her.

The thought of her ex made her frown. She glanced out the window of her RV. She was in a Louisiana rest stop, and it was raining hard. She had pulled off the highway when she lost visibility, and planned to get going again as soon as it cleared up. The dry New Mexico desert seemed like another world entirely. She'd only left the state a couple days ago, and she still woke up every morning thankful for the comforts of her RV.

She had no idea how long Rosemary and Noah were going to spend behind bars. She knew it would be months before they got their sentences handed down, and she probably wouldn't ever know the outcomes unless she wrote to them or it was reported in the news. Thankfully, she did know that Alan would be okay. He had already been awake and aware in the hospital when she left, and his prognosis was good.

In the cage strapped to the passenger seat beside her, Cicero said, "Whatcha doin'?" He fluffed his feathers out and gave her a judgmental look from one pale avian eye.

"I'm just thinking, buddy," Tulia said, smiling over at him. He was none the worse for wear, and had been happy to see her when she returned to the vet clinic. They had been understanding, especially since the rescue had made the news. A team had gone out later the same day to retrieve Ricardo's body, which had thankfully remained undisturbed.

She'd had a lot of calls and messages waiting for

her when she finally got back to civilization. She went through the list, assuring her parents that she was okay, calling the vet, then calling Samuel, who said he'd gotten a hit on Luis's license plate when Luis got a speeding ticket heading south out of San Francisco. Tulia had no doubt that now that she had updated her blog, he would be heading in her general direction, or at least towards New Mexico. Right now, Samuel and her parents were the only ones who knew she was in Louisiana, and she wanted to keep it that way.

She shut the computer off and leaned back in her seat, watching the rain come down. Her trip was more than half over by this point, and she had mixed feelings about it. On the one hand, it would be nice to get home, see her family again, and be back in familiar surroundings. On the other hand, she would miss this, the sense of adventure, always being on the road and seeing something new.

She still didn't know what she wanted to do when she got home, but she could take the time to figure it out. There was no rush. If there was one lesson she had learned so far in her travels, it was to take the time to appreciate the small things. Including the full bottle of water sitting in the RV's cupholder. She was never taking *that* for granted again.

Made in the USA
Coppell, TX
29 October 2023

23577809R00057